JADA JONES

★ SLEEPOVER SCIENTIST ★

Jada Jones

★ SLEEPOVER SCIENTIST ★

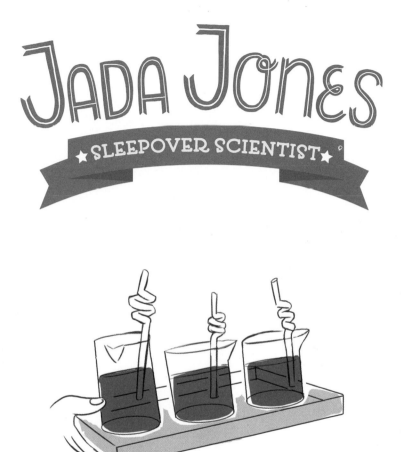

by Kelly Starling Lyons
illustrated by Nneka Myers

Penguin Workshop
An Imprint of Penguin Random House

W

PENGUIN WORKSHOP
Penguin Young Readers Group
An Imprint of Penguin Random House LLC

Text copyright © 2019 by Kelly Starling Lyons. Cover illustration copyright © 2019 by Vanessa Brantley Newton. Illustrations copyright © 2019 by Penguin Random House LLC. All rights reserved. Published by Penguin Workshop, an imprint of Penguin Random House LLC, 345 Hudson Street, New York, New York 10014. PENGUIN and PENGUIN WORKSHOP are trademarks of Penguin Books Ltd, and the W colophon is a registered trademark of Penguin Random House LLC.
Manufactured in China.

Book design by Kayla Wasil.

Library of Congress Cataloging-in-Publication Data is available.

ISBN 9781524790554 (paperback)   10 9 8 7 6 5 4 3 2 1
ISBN 9781524790561 (library binding)   10 9 8 7 6 5 4 3 2 1

For Missy, Stacy, Niche, Shaune,
and best friends everywhere
—KSL

Thank you to my mom, sisters,
and dear friends for your
continuous support that pushes
me to keep going and do my best
even in the hardest of times.
I wouldn't have come this far
without you—NM

Chapter One

THE BIG IDEA

I love school, but long weekends are the best. Dad gets home early. Mom takes off from the library when she can. I plan family adventures, like going to the Museum of Life and Science or visiting Morehead Planetarium.

That's why I was surprised when Mom suggested something else for the one coming up.

"Jada, you're always planning fun for the family, why don't you think of something just for you?"

Yes! I didn't need to think. I looked around my room at the posters of my science heroes, like Dr. Mae Jemison and Dr. George Washington Carver, and knew just what I wanted: my first sleepover. My friends and I could make ice cream in plastic bags, create slime, and do other cool experiments. An evening all about science with my BFFs. Couldn't get any better than that.

"Can I have a sleepover with Lena and Simone, please?"

I crossed my fingers behind my back and waited and hoped . . . and hoped and waited. Seconds felt like hours.

"That's a great idea," Mom said. "Let me talk to your dad."

I crossed my fingers tighter as Mom left my room and headed downstairs. My best friend Mari and I were supposed to have a science sleepover. But then she moved away. So I wanted to have one with my besties from school, Lena and Simone.

Mom came back smiling.

Yes!

"I'll ask their parents," she said. "If it's okay with them, it's fine with Daddy and me."

"Thanks, Mom!" I gave her a hug. "I want to do kitchen chemistry and call it the Best Friends Lab."

"Nice idea, but I didn't know Lena

and Simone were into science like you."

I paused and thought about my friends. Sure, they liked other things more, like jumping double Dutch, writing stories, acting, making arts and crafts. But they didn't *hate* science.

"They like it okay," I said. "But after the sleepover, they'll love it."

"Hmmm," Mom said. "They might. But you might want to have some other activities, too."

I heard what Mom said, but I knew my friends would love my science sleepover. What was there not to like?

I ran to the playroom to get a

white crayon and two pieces of white paper for my invisible message invitations. I wrote them out. Yay! You couldn't see anything. All Simone and Lena had to do was paint on the paper with watercolors for the waxy writing to appear. *Wait until they got their invites*, I thought. *Bet they'd be surprised.*

At school, it was hard to keep my sleepover secret. The invitations were in my backpack. Mom told me to give them out at the end of the day.

"You look happy," Lena said when I sat at our table. "What are you smiling about?"

"You'll see," I answered, then started on my morning work. I tried to focus, but kept thinking about the sleepover. I pictured my friends looking amazed as we did one super science project after another.

"Jada? Jada!"

"Huh?"

I snapped out of my daydream. My classmates giggled.

"Sorry, Miss Taylor," I said.

"Could you please turn in your worksheet?"

How was I going to make it
through the day?

Finally, the last bell rang. As we
headed to the buses and carpool lane,
I handed each of my BFFs a small bag
with a folded piece of white paper and
a plastic palette of watercolor paint.

"What's this?" Simone asked, peeking into the bag. She pulled out the paper and opened it.

"It's an invisible message," I said, beaming. "When you get home, paint the paper with the watercolors and writing will appear."

"Cool!" Lena said.

"I guess," Simone said, crinkling her nose. "Sounds like a lot of work. Can't you just tell us what it says?"

"Simooonnne."

I stuck out my lip and made my eyes as big as I could.

"Okay, okay," she said, laughing. "Just stop with that face. I'll paint it and read."

The next day, sleepovers were the talk of lunch.

"I've only had sleepovers with my cousins," Lena said. "We're going to have so much fun."

"I have to admit, the invitation was pretty cool," Simone said.

"What are you talking about?" Gabi asked.

"Sleepovers."

"Oh," she said. "The last one I

had was terrible. One of my friends didn't like the snacks I picked out. My cousin didn't want to play games. She kept complaining about being bored and wanted to go home. I just wanted it to be over."

That sounded awful. I hoped ours wouldn't be like that.

"I had a sleepover for my birthday," Miles said, digging into his mac and cheese. "It was great until we got into a fight over a video game. One person didn't talk for hours."

I hadn't thought about sleepover problems. What if mine was a flop? My leg bobbed up and down as I tried to push that thought out of my mind.

"So what are we going to do at the sleepover?" Simone asked as we waited to jump rope at recess.

"It's a surprise," I said. "I have it all planned."

"Oooh, do you want me to bring my nail polish? I got a new set with sparkly colors," Simone said. "Check it out."

She wiggled her fingers to show off her violet nails that looked like a sky filled with stars.

"I can bring my speaker so we can listen to music," Lena added.

They traded ideas back and forth: Karaoke. Games. Drawing. Every time they came up with a new suggestion, my stomach fluttered like a bird trying to break free. Not once did they mention anything related to science. I thought about the sleepover disasters we talked about at lunch. I hoped my big idea didn't turn into a big bust. I forced myself to show my brightest smile.

"All you have to do is show up," I said. "Leave the fun to me."

Chapter Two:
SURPRISE GUESTS

At home, I scanned the books on our shelves until I found the one I was looking for: *Home Science Experiments.* I curled up on the couch, flipped through the pages, and started thinking about projects that could make Simone and Lena science fans like me. Just when I opened my notebook to write down a few ideas, my little brother, Jackson, walked in.

"Can I come to your sleepover?"

"No, sorry, Jax. It's girls only."

"No fair," he said, stomping his foot and pouting. "I like science, too."

"I know," I said. "But we do science together all the time. At the sleepover, I want to do it with my friends."

"No fair!" He stomped again. "Simone and Lena are my friends, too. I'm telling Mom.

"Mom!" he yelled, running into the next room.

Great. Now I had little brother drama. I sighed and started working on my list. Simone mentioned painting nails. I saw an experiment using clear nail polish to make rainbow art. Maybe they'd like that. Lena talked about music. What if we jammed while we made science magic? I smiled, leaned back against a fluffy pillow, and exhaled. I had it covered. Nothing to worry about.

Mom came in with Jax right behind her.

"Jada, would it hurt for Jax to be there for a little bit of the sleepover? Maybe he could do the first experiment. Then, it could be just the girls."

I sighed again.

"I really don't think . . ."

Mom gave me a look that meant to keep my thoughts to myself.

"Just the first one."

Jax pumped his fist and pulled it down to his side. He flapped his knees like a football player scoring a touchdown.

"I get to go! I get to go!"

I frowned. I was glad he was happy. I sure wasn't.

★

On sleepover day, Daddy took me to the discount store to get plastic tablecloths, plates, bowls, and food for kitchen science. I dragged behind as we walked up and down the aisles. I found everything on my list and then spotted decorations with atoms, the periodic table of elements, magnifying glasses, and microscopes. It was just what I wanted, but I couldn't get excited.

"Look, Jada!" Daddy said. "How about these for your sleepover?"

"Sure. Thanks," I said, and dropped them into the cart without a smile.

"Now I know something is wrong," he said, hugging my shoulder. "Aren't you excited?"

"Kinda," I said. "A little nervous too. I hope everyone has fun."

"They will, baby girl," he said. "They're your friends. You don't have to worry or do anything fancy to entertain them. Just be you."

At home, I taped the "Best Friends Lab" banner on the wall in the kitchen. I decorated the table and cabinets with colorful science pictures—flasks filled with bubbling yellow and purple liquid, blue and green atoms on a background of orange. I grouped the supplies for each activity and put the bowls in the middle. I set out safety goggles for party favors. I wanted everything to be just right.

"When are Lena and Simone coming?" Jax asked.

"At seven."

"Yay!"

I sighed and headed to my room to rest before the big evening. I lay down on my daybed and closed my eyes. When I opened them and looked at the clock, it was almost time for the fun to start. I rushed downstairs, sat on the couch, and waited for the doorbell or a knock. Nothing. I checked out the supplies. Everything was in place. I sat on the couch and waited some more. Crickets.

I walked to the window and opened the blinds. No one was coming up our steps. No cars were driving toward our house. I sank onto the couch and felt my last drop of hope fading as I waited. I got up and peeked one last time. The street was empty. I walked up the stairs to my room and realized this was worse than I imagined. My sleepover wouldn't be a disaster; it wouldn't happen at all.

I sat up in bed, startled as the doorbell echoed through the house.

My heart pounded. Sweat dampened my forehead. I looked at the clock— 6 p.m. I inhaled and breathed out slowly. Whew. It had just been a nightmare. My sleepover didn't start for another hour.

"Jada," Daddy called. "It's for you."

I jumped up and raced down the steps toward the door. I wondered who came early—Lena or Simone. Daddy had a funny grin when I passed him.

I blinked, shook my head, blinked again, and then screamed.

"Mari!"

We jumped up and down. I hugged her so tight, I wondered if she could breathe. I couldn't believe

my bestie wasn't in Phoenix. She was right here in Raleigh, standing in front of me.

"How? When? What are you doing here?"

We laughed.

"My Aunt Tasha is getting married on Saturday."

"Why didn't you tell me?"

I hugged her again. I had to make sure she was real.

"I wanted to surprise you."

"I'm having a sleepover tonight. Can you come?"

"Yep." She picked up her lavender overnight bag and grinned. "Your mom told mine all about it."

"Really? This is going to be the

best sleepover ever! Wait until Lena and Simone see you."

I pinched my arm to make sure I wasn't dreaming again. My three best friends together. What could go wrong?

Chapter Three:

I pulled Mari into the kitchen.

"I love your hair!" I said.

It was in a braided updo for the wedding.

"Thank you," she said. "I love your lab!"

She oohed and aahed as she looked at everything I had set out on the island for our activities: laundry detergent, liquid glue, clear nail polish, strips of black construction paper. The kitchen table was covered with a plastic purple tablecloth and ready for action.

"You have the best ideas!" she said. "Tonight is going to be superrific."

I missed her crazy words. Mari always made me smile. It was so cool that we'd have our science sleepover together after all.

"I can't believe you're here," I said, plopping on a stool. "How's Arizona?"

"I miss you so much," she said. "But I'm making friends and we do day trips on weekends. My favorite so far is Sedona."

"Is that the postcard you sent me of the red rocks?"

"Yep, they're everywhere. When the sun sets, it looks like the rocks are glowing. I have pictures on my tablet."

"Cool! Let's save those until Simone and Lena get here."

Jax and Mom came in.

"Mari!"

Jax ran to her.

"Hey, Action Jackson," she said, rubbing his head.

"Good to have you back, Mari," Mom said, giving her a hug.

I filled Mari in on our class and science club and showed her a new treasure I added to my rock and mineral collection: agate with patterns of swirls.

"Marvtastic!" Mari said as she admired it.

It felt good having her back.

Right at seven, the doorbell rang again.

"Stay in here," I told Mari. "Let's keep the surprise going."

I ran to the door and peeked through the blinds.

"Lena!"

I swung it open and put her flowered bag next to Mari's. As Mom talked to her mom, I told Lena to close her eyes. I led her by the hand into the living room.

"Okay, you can look."

She stared and opened her mouth. Nothing came out. Then, finally she squeaked, "Mari?"

"Hey, Lena," Mari said, giving her a hug.

"Mari's here for the weekend. Isn't that awesome?"

Lena and Mari caught up, talking about school and friends. Now, all we needed was Simone. A few minutes later, the doorbell rang again.

"Why don't you answer the door this time, Mari?" I said. "That will definitely surprise her."

Lena and I watched as Mari walked to the entryway with Mom behind her. She peeked through the blinds and saw Simone, then opened the door.

"Wait, what?" I heard Simone say. "Mari? What are you doing here?"

"Surprise!" she said and held out her arms.

Simone looked stunned, like she didn't know what to do.

"Group hug," I screamed.

Lena and I raced down the hall to join them.

"Aren't you going to invite Simone in?" Mom asked.

I laughed.

"Oh yeah, come on in. Let's get this party started."

Everyone followed me into the kitchen. I turned and spread my arms wide in a big flourish.

"Welcome to the Best Friends Lab. Can't believe I have my three BFFs here with me. This will be the best night ever."

"Wow, Jada," Simone said, checking out the decorations. "This is a lot of . . . science. Cool lab."

"Yeah, it looks amazing," Lena said.

"Why don't we jump into our first experiment?"

I put the bowl of M&M's and a pitcher of water on the table.

"Everyone grab a plate and a cup."

Jax rushed into the room.

"Did you start without me?"

"No, Jax, we're just setting up. I have your plate and cup right here. He's going to do one experiment with us. Then, he's leaving. Right, Jax?"

"Right," he said, looking down and sounding like he wasn't so sure.

I showed everyone how to line up the candy around the inside circle of the plate. Then, I poured water into everyone's cups.

"Just pour into the middle of the plate," I said. "The water just needs to touch the candy. You don't need a lot."

Jax popped an M&M into his mouth.

"Yum," he said. "One for the plate. One for me. One for the plate. One for me ..."

"You're going to eat up your experiment, Jax. You can have some of the extras when we're done."

"Sorry." He finally finished his circle and started to slowly add the water.

"Now what do we do?" Simone said.

"Wait." Mari and I giggled when we said it together.

"You want something to drink?" I asked. I grabbed punch out of the refrigerator. It was in cups that looked like beakers with crazy straws.

As the candy coating on the M&M's dissolved, the colors began to streak until they met in the middle.

"It's so pretty!" Lena said.

"Why is mine taking so long?"

Jax said, not realizing that since he finished later it would take longer for the coating to dissolve into rainbow streams. "I think it needs more water."

"No, Jax!" I said, but I wasn't fast enough.

He picked up the pitcher and couldn't handle it. Water gushed everywhere. Everyone jumped away

from the table. But our experiments were ruined. The M&M's in the bowl were soaked. So much for extras.

"Jax!"

"It was an accident!"

"I know," I said. "It's okay. Why don't you go upstairs with Daddy and Mom? I think they have something special for you to do."

"I want to stay here," he whined.

I sighed. I knew this was coming.

"I'll be right back," I said to my friends. I came back down with Daddy.

Mari, Simone, and Lena were wiping up the mess.

"Thanks so much for cleaning up," I said.

"That's what you call keepers,"
Daddy said.

Everyone smiled.

"After all that hard work, are you
girls ready for pizza?"

"Yes," we said together.

"Great, I'll place the order. Come
upstairs, Jax. You, Mom, and I will
have our own sleepover. We have
your Black Panther action figures

ready in your room."

"Wakanda forever!" he screamed. "But it's still no fair that Jada gets to have all the friend fun."

Little brothers.

"Who wants to have ice cream before the pizza?" I asked.

"Now you're talking," Simone said, raising her hand.

"Grab two plastic bags. One little and one big. I'll get the ice, salt, and half-and-half."

Simone frowned. "Where's the ice cream?"

"We're going to make it, silly," Mari said, smiling.

Simone looked at Lena, who gazed at the floor.

"Everything tonight isn't going to be a science project, is it? Can't we just eat the ice cream without learning about it?" Simone asked.

I felt that bird-trying-to-escape flutter in my stomach again. Why didn't Simone give science a chance? I looked at Lena. She didn't complain, but she wasn't smiling, either. Mari looked at my face and jumped right in.

"I scream, you scream, we all scream for ice cream," she sang and struck a silly pose. "If you don't want yours, Simone, that's more for me."

Simone laughed.

"How do we do this, Jada?" Lena asked.

"Wait, Lena, we have to get into character," Simone grabbed goggles from the island and struck a pose.

"Scientist Simone, reporting for duty."

We laughed and each grabbed a

pair. We didn't need the goggles for the experiment, but I didn't care. We were finally having fun.

"Okay, you put half-and-half, vanilla extract, and sugar in the small plastic bag," I said, showing them how as they followed my lead. "You can add chocolate syrup or strawberries if you want, too. Fill the gallon bag halfway with ice. Add the salt. Seal the small bag real tight and put it into the gallon bag. Seal that, too. Okay, now all we have to do is shake."

I hit the music. Beyoncé's voice filled the room. It was *on* after that. Simone and Lena made up a shake-the-bag dance. Simone shook it high. Lena shook it low. Mari shook it side to side. I shook it behind my back. Everyone was having fun until . . .

"Ahhhh!" Lena screamed as half-and-half spewed everywhere. It was on her clothes, on the floor, on the counter. "I'm all wet!"

"Oh no, your bags must not have been closed all the way! I'll get some paper towels," I told her.

"I don't want ice cream anymore," Lena said.

"Me either," Simone said.

I couldn't blame them. I remembered

Daddy telling
me about
something
called Murphy's
Law. It says
whatever can
go wrong will
go wrong. I
think they
should rename
it Jada's Law,
because that's
what was happening. My sleepover
was turning into a mess.

Chapter Four:
STALEMATE

"What happened?" Mom said, racing into the room.

"Lena's bag spilled."

"I see," she said, staring at the mess. "Why don't you girls put on your pj's while we clean up."

I helped Mom while my friends took turns changing.

"Things not going so great?" Mom

said, looking at me.

"Not at all," I said while mopping up the floor with paper towels. "Everything is going wrong."

"Why don't you ask them what they want to do? They might have some ideas."

I thought about what Mom said.

Maybe tonight didn't have to be all about science.

After I changed into my purple pajamas, the pizza arrived. We sat around the dining room table and ate in silence. Time to try something new.

"So what do you want to do next?" I asked.

"Not science," Simone said.

"We don't have to," I said. "We can do anything."

"Do you want to sing?" Lena asked. "We can take turns, pretending we're onstage."

"Sure," I said.

We sang songs from Disney movies, and R&B and pop hits. We

acted out music videos. It felt good having fun with my girls. I heard a giggle and saw eyes peeking from the stairs. I didn't need to see the whole face to know who it was.

"Jax!"

He ran up the steps. Things were back to normal.

"Okay, Mari, your pick. What do you want to do?"

"I saw you have an experiment with nail polish."

"Not more science," Simone said, and groaned.

"You'll like this one," I said. "Promise."

Mom and I had practiced a few times before they arrived. We made sure to do the experiment quickly and that the room had good air flow so the nail polish smell wouldn't be overwhelming. I did the same as I showed my friends how it worked. I opened the clear nail polish and let a couple drops hit the water. Then, I laid the black paper on the surface, pulled it out, and laid it on a paper towel to dry. A swirl of colors burst across it.

"Wow," Lena said. "That's like a work of art."

She tried it next. It turned out just right. Mari's worked out great, too. But Simone was having trouble.

First, she left the paper in too long. Then, she put the paper in the wrong spot. I dropped in more nail polish so she could try again.

"This is no fun," Simone said.

"You almost have it," Mari said. "Try it one more time."

"Easy for you to say, Mari," Simone said. "You love science. The old friends are back together, so who cares what we think, right?"

"That's not fair, Simone," I said. "You're all my friends."

"It doesn't feel like it tonight."

"Forget it," I said. "We can do something else. What do you want to do?"

"Play truth or dare," she said.

"Okay."

"Lena, truth or dare?"

"Truth."

"Are you having fun at Jada's party?"

Lena didn't say anything.

"You have to answer."

"Not really," she said, and stared at the floor. "Sorry, Jada."

"I'm sorry, too," I said, feeling tears pool in my eyes. "I just wanted to share my favorite thing with my favorite friends!"

"But we're not in school, Jada," Simone said. "We came here to hang out with you and have fun."

"What's going on, girls?" Mom said. "I heard you from upstairs. Looks like you could use a break. How about a movie?"

We nodded and headed into the family room. I turned on the channel with the options.

Figures. We all liked something different.

"Why don't we take a vote?" Simone said.

She and Lena picked the animated movie. Mari and I raised

our hands for the live-action fantasy one.

Split down the middle, just like my heart. This wasn't working out.

"How about we flip a coin," Mari suggested. "Heads, we watch the Disney movie. Tails, we watch the dragon one."

Tails, Mari and I won. But why did it feel like losing?

Chapter Five:
END OF THE ROAD

The movie was on, but no one was watching. Simone looked at Lena, who glanced back at her. She dug her toe into the carpet and made a groove like she wished she could carve a path to get out. Neither said a word.

I got up from the floor where I was stretched out.

"Do you want some popcorn?" I asked.

Mari nodded. Lena shrugged. Simone didn't answer at all.

I walked into the kitchen and put the bag of popcorn in the microwave. I watched it getting bigger and bigger. It reminded me of us. Our problems just kept growing. I wondered how long it would take for things to explode.

I put the popcorn in bowls and passed them around.

"Thank you," Simone said.

We just sat there, not watching the movie, not smiling, not looking at one another.

I picked up the remote and hit the off button.

"What's wrong, Simone?"

"I don't want to hurt your feelings, Jada," she said. "But this is lame. First, we had to do all that science. Then, you turned on a movie we didn't want to see."

"I thought science would be fun," I said.

"Not for Lena and me!" Simone snapped.

Maybe the silence was better.

"I didn't want to cause trouble," Mari said. "Maybe I shouldn't have come over. Can I call my mom?"

"No, Mari, please don't leave."

"You stay, Mari," Lena said. "You and Jada love science. I can go."

"Me too," Simone said. "Jada already has everything she needs with her real best friend here."

I couldn't believe all of my friends wanted to leave. My happiest day ever was turning into my worst. The sleepover was crashing fast. What was I going to do?

Chapter Six

FORMULA FOR FUN

"**L**ook, let's start over," I said. My friends frowned like it was too late.

"Can we play a game? Two truths and a lie?" I asked. "I will forget about science for the rest of the night. I will be happy if you leave. I don't care what we do as long as we're together."

Simone was the first to smile.

"Okay, Jada," she said. "But if we're going to play, let's play for real. My turn. I'm going to be a famous TV reporter one day. I'm going to win a double Dutch tournament. I'm going to be mad if we don't do some more science."

"Very funny," I said. "Lena, you're up."

We kept going back and forth, making up sillier and sillier lies until we were cracking up on the floor.

"Okay, ladies," Mom said, smiling as she saw us having fun together. "It's midnight. Time for bed."

Mari looked at me and whispered in my ear. I grinned and whispered to Simone, who shared with Lena.

"Uh-oh, looks like a plan is in motion," Mom said. "What's up?"

"Can we *please* make a fort, Ms. Keisha?" Mari said.

"Hmmm," Mom said, thinking it over. "I guess every sleepover needs one."

She winked and left.

"Yes!" we shouted, and got busy putting it together. Lena laid a fuzzy blanket on the floor. Simone suggested using kitchen chairs for the frame. Mari draped them with a patterned comforter. I ran upstairs to get more sheets and pillows.

We put pillows inside and a few stuffed animals. We stood back and admired what we had built.

"It's wondermazing!" Mari said. I nodded my head. That sounded just right. It was the best fort I ever saw.

We made the perfect team.

I crawled inside with my three best friends and knew there was no place I'd rather be.

"Mom said, 'Time for bed,' but she didn't say we had to go to sleep."

We giggled and whispered until one by one my friends' voices were replaced with steady breathing. As I closed my eyes, I knew I would have good dreams that night.

Chapter Seven:

SLEEPOVER SURVIVORS

I n the morning, I was the first one up. I smiled as I looked at my friends sleeping side by side. I slid out of our fort as quietly as I could and stretched.

"So you survived your first sleepover," Daddy said softly. "How do you feel?"

"Hungry."

He laughed.

"Pancakes?"

I nodded.

"One sleepover special pancake and waffle bar on the way," he said.

By the time my friends got up, he had everything ready: banana pancakes and sweet potato waffles. Dishes of berries, jars of sprinkles, and a can of whipped cream sat on the table.

"Yum," we all said together.

We ate at the dining room table and played two truths and a lie some more.

"I'll start," Mari said. "I'm going to miss you all when I leave. I'm glad I got to come back. I hope you forget about me."

"Never, Mari," I said.

"Yep," Simone said. "You're stuck with us."

Lena smiled. "Best friends forever."

"Mari, why don't you show them your pictures?" I said. Mari grabbed her tablet. We smiled at photos of her with her cousins in Sedona and at the Grand Canyon.

We gave her a group hug. "Are you

all done with your science supplies?"
Mom asked.

Before I could say yes, Simone
jumped in.

"Do we have time for one more
experiment before we leave?"

"What?"

Mari, Lena, and I looked at one
another. Was that really Simone?

"I know I complained, but some of
those projects were kinda cool."

"I think you have time for one more," Mom said.

After we cleaned our plates and helped clear the table, I spread out another plastic tablecloth and got the liquid laundry detergent and glue.

I passed out bowls and spoons to all my friends and set out one extra. Jax kept inching closer and closer. He thought I didn't see him. But I motioned with my finger for him to come over.

"Want to make slime with us? There's a spot for you right next to me."

"Thank you, Jada!" he said, and hugged me tight. Mom watched to make sure we did everything safely as I gave the instructions.

"First we add a third of a cup of glue to the bowl. Next, we add a tablespoon of laundry soap. If it's too sticky, add a little more detergent. Then, knead it with your fingers until it's just like you want."

"You have glitter glue!" Simone said.

"Of course," I said. "Got it just for you."

We mixed the glue and liquid detergent together. Slowly, it started to gel. This time, everyone's turned out right.

"It's gross but cool at the same time," Simone said as she stretched hers. It looked like sparkling taffy.

"I can't stop pulling it." Soon, the parents started arriving. I gave everyone tubs to take their slime with them. We hugged and said goodbye. But the best keepsake wouldn't fit in a container.

We posed for a picture before they left. Jax jumped in right before it was snapped.

"Photobomb!" he screamed.

We laughed. That was the perfect picture to capture our wacky time.

My first sleepover was tough, but I did it with my three best friends. This was a memory that would stick with me forever. I couldn't wait until we had a sleepover again.

JADA'S RULES FOR BEING A SLEEPOVER SCIENTIST

1. Be safe. Always get permission for experiments. Ask a parent or guardian to supervise.

2. Think with your heart and your mind.

3. Consider the opinions of others.

4. Keep trying to get it right.

5. Create your own formula for fun.

ACKNOWLEDGMENTS

To all of the amazing Jada Jones readers, thank you for your sweet notes, pictures, reviews, and support. You've made the debut of this series incredible. I'm touched by how you've connected with Jada and her friends. You inspire me.

I'm so grateful, too, for the editors who believed in Jada and me. Thank you, Renee Hooker, for your expert guidance and kind support through all of Jada's adventures. Thank you, Bonnie Bader and Avery Briggs, for starting the magic. Hugs and thanks to the entire Penguin Workshop team, illustrators Vanessa Brantley Newton and Nneka Myers, and my agent Caryn Wiseman.

Finally, thank you always to my family, sorors, and friends. I couldn't do this without you.

And now, here's a sneak peek at the next

JADA JONES

★ DANCING QUEEN ★

"Today, we're changing gym class to dance class to kick off the fun," Mr. Best said. Soon, the sounds of the line dance the Cupid Shuffle echoed in the room.

"Follow me."

Mr. Best led us through the steps, one at a time. Walking to the right, I could do that. Walking to the left, okay. Kicking then walking and turning. This wasn't so bad. But when it was time to put it all together, that's when things fell apart. Every time the line turned, I was a beat behind. I bumped into someone. I tripped over my feet. I was lost. I moved to the back and hoped nobody caught my stumbles. Thankfully, the bell rang and set me free.

Simone and Lena didn't seem to notice.

"You know we have to do the challenge together," Simone said.

"Yeah," Lena said. "This is going to be awesome."

I smiled and nodded even though my head was throbbing. They were my best friends, but no way could I keep up with them. What was I going to do?

In class, Miss Taylor passed out the kindness checklists and pledge sheets. The more sponsors we signed up and dances we tried, the more money we could raise. No one would keep track of what dances we completed. It was up to us to be honest.

I scanned the list of dances the Council Crew came up with: the Cupid Shuffle, Whip and Nae Nae, Chicken Dance, the Floss. It went on and on. As I read each one, I felt the jitters jamming in my stomach.